Mother Goose of Yesteryear

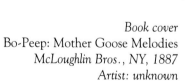

Book cover
Old King Cole: Mother Goose Melodies
McLoughlin Bros., NY, 1888
Artist: unknown

Book cover
Bo-Peep: Mother Goose Melodies
McLoughlin Bros., NY, 1887
Artist: unknown

Mother Goose of Yesteryear

Barbara Hallman Kissinger

PELICAN PUBLISHING COMPANY
GRETNA 2008

The word "Pelican" and the depiction of a pelican
are trademarks of Pelican Publishing Company, Inc.,
and are registered in the U.S. Patent and Trademark Office.

Library of Congress Cataloging-in-Publication Data

Kissinger, Barbara Hallman.
  Mother Goose of yesteryear / Barbara Hallman Kissinger.
      p. cm.
  Includes indexes.
  ISBN-13: 978-1-58980-557-6 (hardcover : alk. paper) 1. Mother Goose—Illustrations. 2. Illustration
of books. 3. Commercial art. I. Title.
  NC961.7.N87K57 2008
  741.6'42—dc22
                                                    2008014145

"Old King Cole," on page 41 and back cover; "Pat-a-Cake, Pat-a-Cake," on page 71; and "Inside cover
illustration of Mother Goose," on title page: from MOTHER GOOSE RHYMES, illustrated by C. M.
Burd, copyright 1927, renewed 1954 by Platt & Munk Company, illustrations. Used by permission of
Platt & Munk, Publishers, A Division of Penguin Young Readers Group, A Member of Penguin Group
(USA) Inc., 345 Hudson Street, New York, NY 10014. All rights reserved.

Printed in China

Published by Pelican Publishing Company, Inc.
1000 Burmaster Street, Gretna, Louisiana 70053

This book is dedicated to all the lovers of Mother Goose.
May she dwell in our hearts and minds forever.

The Old Mother Goose Nursery Rhyme Book
Thomas Nelson & Sons, 1926
Artist: Anne Anderson

Book cover
Mother Goose ABC Book
M. A. Donohue & Co., Chicago, n.d.
Artist: unknown

Book cover
Gems from Mother Goose
Rhymes, Chimes and Jingles
McLoughlin Bros., NY, 1898
Artist: unknown

CONTENTS

Mother Goose and her Nursery Rhymes in . . .

Book cover
Mother Goose, as Told by Father Gander
George M. Hill Company, n.d., ca. 1895
Artist: unknown

Book cover
The Complete Mother Goose
The Saalfield Publishing Co., 1915
Artist: Frances Brundage

INTRODUCTION

Who hasn't heard of Mother Goose? As adults, we remember some of the more popular nursery rhyme lines: "Mary had a little lamb, Jack and Jill went up the hill," or "Humpty Dumpty sat on a wall." But most of us can't quite remember our mothers reading those rhymes to us because we were so young. It might be said that Mother Goose, herself, repeated those old nursery jingles to us over and over again. Was it really Mother Goose's hand that rocked the cradle?

There is not much known about the history of Mother Goose, and this book is not going to discuss the origins of Mother Goose, except through some of the old Mother Goose illustrations of the late nineteenth and early twentieth centuries in America.

Mother Goose of Yesteryear deals mostly with the art of book illustrations of long ago and the nursery rhymes that were being illustrated at that time. Also included are antique trade cards, postcards, newspapers, and magazine illustrations of the late nineteenth and early twentieth centuries. Mother Goose was symbolized as either having a witchlike appearance, wearing bright colored clothing, or as an anthropomorphic goose, whom children gathered around to listen to her recitation of nursery rhymes and tales. All in all she was a storyteller, and a good one at that.

A few of her books began appearing in the late eighteenth and early nineteenth centuries, and by the end of the nineteenth century, they were becoming very popular. Many of the early illustrations were drawn anonymously. Book publishers didn't give the illustrators of these drawings any recognition, and it wasn't until after the turn of the twentieth century that artists began to gain acknowledgment. The Golden Age of Illustration began in the 1880s and lasted until the 1920s. Some of the more identifiable artists of that time are: Kate Greenaway, Walter Crane, Ethel Franklin Betts, Fanny Cory, Blanche Fisher Wright, Ella Dolbear Lee, Clara M. Burd, Frances Brundage, Chester Van Nortwick, Frederick Richardson, Eulalie Lenski, and Arthur Rackham. Even Johnny Gruelle of Raggedy Ann fame illustrated a Mother Goose

Book cover
Mother Goose
Sam'l Gabriel Sons & Co., 1915
Artist: A. M. Turner

book, as well as Jesse Willcox Smith. You will come across many of these artists in this book.

Mother Goose of Yesteryear contains a lot of old nursery rhymes in the Rhyme Time section of this book. Of course, I couldn't come any where close to including all the nursery jingles of old. As nursery rhymes were passed down through the centuries, some of the wording seemed to change, so you may not remember the rhymes as you learned them. Some of the jingles were crass in the focus of their rhymes; the old woman who lived in the shoe would probably be charged with child abuse today.

I hope you will enjoy and appreciate the vintage illustrations and pass this book on to your children as a reminder of the Mother Goose of yesteryear. So that Mother Goose and her nursery rhymes will be remembered in our hearts forever.

Frontispiece
Mother Goose's Melodies Set to Music
McLoughlin Bros., NY, n.d.
Artist: Ernest Grispe

The Only True Mother Goose Melodies:
An Exact Reproduction of the Text and
Illustrations of the Original Edition
Lothrop, Lee & Shepard Co., Boston, 1905
By Munroe & Frances
Artist: unknown

NINETEENTH CENTURY BOOKS

Mother Goose in America was associated with a grand-motherly figure, not handsome in any way in appearance, who had children gathered around her. Above is an engraver's idea of Mother Goose in the early nineteenth century.

In the 1880s and '90s, printing companies used the chromolithography process for producing very colorful books. Publishing quite a few Mother Goose books, McLoughlin Brothers, Inc. of New York became the largest manufacturer of picture books for children by the 1870s. McLoughlin produced higher quality books as far as images were concerned than other publishers of the late nineteenth century.

On the facing page is a frontispiece for the book *Mother Goose's Melodies Set to Music*, by J. W. Elliott, ca.

1870s, produced by McLoughlin. It included a number of figures from nursery rhymes the reader might recognize. Some of the images included in this book by Elliott are pictured on pages 12 and 13.

While Mother Goose books are usually associated with nursery rhymes, her books didn't always include them; some were adventures of her life. She even appeared from time to time with Santa Claus. An illustration from one such book titled *Mother Goose's Ball* is included at the end of this section. Another example of a little different approach to Mother Goose is the book *Mother Goose, as Told by Father Gander*. A frontispiece of this book is on the last page of this section. Mother Goose seemed to acquire a husband at some time or another, just as Santa found Mrs. Claus.

"Little Bo-Peep"

Mother Goose article illustration
Scribner's Monthly, *December 1872*

"Man in the Moon"

Mother Goose article illustration
Scribner's Monthly, *December 1872*

"Mistress Mary, Quite Contrary"

Mother Goose's Melodies Set to Music
First published ca. 1871
McLoughlin Bros., NY, n.d.
Artist: unknown

"Little Jack Horner"

Mother Goose's Melodies Set to Music
First published ca. 1871
McLoughlin Bros., NY, n.d.

There were about six books that came out in the late 1870s by G. W. Carleton & Co. of New York. They were called *Mother Goose Melodies with Magic Colored Pictures* (also titled *The Old Fashioned Mother Goose Melodies, Complete, with Magic Colored Pictures*) or *with Magical Changes*. The first picture would be folded to look like a regular illustration; then one would open up the page to its full width to see a different illustration, as shown on these pages.

Folded picture of "Sing a Song of Sixpence"

Mother Goose Melodies with Magical Changes
G. W. Carleton & Co., 1879
Artist: W.L.S.

Unfolded picture of "Sing a Song of Sixpence"

Folded picture of "Little Miss Muffet"

Mother Goose Melodies with Magical Changes
also titled: The Old Fashioned
Mother Goose Melodies Complete
with Magic Colored Pictures
G. W. Carleton & Co., NY, 1879
Artist: W.L.S.

Unfolded picture of "Little Miss Muffet"

Book illustration
Mother Goose's Ball
D. Lothrop Company, Boston, 1893
Artist: unknown

Frontispiece: Father Gander
Mother Goose, as Told by Father Gander
George M. Hill Company, n.d., ca. 1895
Artist: unknown

A Merry Christmas
from Harper's Weekly
January 3, 1880
Artist: Thomas Nast

Old Mother Goose Melodies

from Thomas Nast's Christmas Drawings for
the Human Race, *ca. 1890*
Artist: Thomas Nast

NEWSPAPERS AND MAGAZINES

Mother Goose and her nursery rhymes not only graced the pages of the early books, but also the newspapers of the nineteenth century and the magazines of the twentieth century. Many illustrations were created by the well-known artists of this period.

Thomas Nast, a political cartoonist for the newspaper *Harper's Weekly* in the late nineteenth century, was one of these illustrators. He was well-known for his depictions of Santa Claus and political figures of the time. He was also responsible for the symbols of the political parties—the elephant for the Republicans and the donkey for the Democrats. On the facing page, his interpretation of Mother Goose and Santa come together in a dancing jig in Mother Goose Land.

The above illustration is one he created around 1874 titled *Old Mother Goose Melodies*, depicting her playing the piano encircled by her beloved children. This was around the time Mother Goose and her jingles came to the forefront of the Victorian family nursery. Nast later published it in his 1890 book *Thomas Nast's Christmas Drawings for the Human Race*.

Featured on the next few pages are Mother Goose illustrations that appeared in nineteenth-century newspapers. These drawings showcase the works of well-known artists of the period. Also included is a magazine illustration from 1923, just after the end of the Golden Age of Illustration (1880-1920).

A ROYAL NURSERY RHYME FOR 1860.

"There was a Royal Lady that lived in a shoe,
She had so many children she didn't know what to do."

A Royal Nursery Rhyme for 1860

from Punch *magazine, ca. 1844*
Artist: John Leech

John Leech (1817-1864) was probably most famous for his 1843 illustrations for Charles Dickens' book *A Christmas Carol*. He was also a cartoonist and illustrator for *Punch* magazine of Britain, which was first published in 1841. One of these cartoons appears above and refers to Queen Victoria of England's childbearing.

Nursery Rhymes

from Harper's Young People
November 15, 1881
Artist: Kate Greenaway

Kate Greenaway (1846-1901) was a famous artist and illustrator. Her father John Greenaway was a wood engraver, who made sure his daughter received an education in the arts. She illustrated the book *Mother Goose*, which was published in 1881. Her illustrations of the nursery rhymes were deemed classic, and *Nursery Rhymes* (above) is a newspaper illustration taken from that book.

"When Mother Goose Dusts Off the Moon,
You'll Know It Will Be Snowing Soon"

from Harper's Young People
March 3, 1885
Artist: Peter Newell

Peter Newell (1862-1924) was a well-known free-lance illustrator at the turn of the century. He did creative works for the *Harper's* publications of the time.

The above illustration is a humorous one of Mother Goose and the crescent-shaped man in the moon.

Simple Simon Has His Day

Illustrations by
Gertrude A. Kay

(The story of Simple Simon is on page 28.)

DIRECTIONS

Paste the entire page on a piece of very heavy wrapping paper, and when the paste is dry cut out the various figures around the outside, dark outline. To make Simple Simon stand, cut the base on which he stands into three parts, bending forward on the red dotted line, and back on the blue dotted lines. To make the goose stand, bend back on the blue dotted lines. Run your scissors between the double dark lines at the top of the stirrup and on the goose's back; then put Mother Goose's foot into the opening above the stirrup and insert the tab on her skirt into the opening on the goose's back. When she sits on the stool push the tab on her skirt through the double dark lines of the opening which is to be cut between the legs of the stool.

from The Ladies Home Journal
April 1923
Artist: Gertrude A. Kay

Several of the magazines of the day had nursery rhyme stories accompanied by figures to assemble. The children, after reading the story on the opposite side, would cut this page out of the magazine and put it together according to the directions. The example above is a paper-doll-type collectible of a story called "Simple Simon Has His Day." Along with him is Mother Goose.

Victorian Nursery Rhyme Trade Cards

"The Queen of Hearts"

Liberty Breakfast Java Coffee, ca. 1890
Artist: unknown

"Little Miss Muffet"

Advertising back

J & P Coats Thread, ca. 1890
Artists: unknown

"Hark! The dogs do bark"

"Mary had a little lamb"
Lutted's S. P. Cough Drops
1882
Artist: unknown

"John, John (Tom, Tom) the Piper's Son"
The Standard Sewing Machine Co.
ca. 1890
Artist: unknown

ADVERTISING EPHEMERA

Advertising cards came about during the late eighteenth century. These probably were a forerunner of the business cards of today. Tradesmen of the day used them to tell locals about their services and expertise. However, it wasn't until about a century later (1880s) that the fascinating, illustrative, and beautifully colored trade cards of the Victorian era became popular.

This rise in popularity was due to the printing process known as chromolithography. The colors produced by this process were vibrant and dazzling. These trade cards were eagerly collected by the ladies and children of the house. The cards were always free and sometimes came inserted as a premium in food products such as coffee and cereal. The illustrations were on the front of the trade card and an advertisement of the product on the back. Some cards allotted a space on the front for the store's name, where they were handed out for free to advertise the particular merchant's wares.

Trade card illustrations included many subjects and seasons. For the purpose of this book, I have concentrated on Mother Goose and her nursery rhymes. If the trade card included the nursery rhyme it depicted, the wording might have been changed to include the product advertised. Sometimes the store advertiser just changed the wording for their own pleasure.

New England Mince Meat
ca. 1890s
Artist: unknown

McLoughlin's XXXX Coffee, ca. 1880-1890s
Artist: unknown

Advertising trade-card paper dolls of Mother Goose and some nursery rhyme figures grace these two pages. These, of course, were very popular with children.

Collectors should really be appreciative if they find dolls that have survived the playful handling by children's little fingers.

Victorian Nursery Rhyme Trade Card Paper Dolls

"Little Boy Blue"

"Little Bo-Peep"

Lion Coffee, ca. 1890
Artists: unknown

"Old Mother Hubbard"

"Little Jack Horner"

Star Soap Co.
ca. 1890
Artist: unknown

4

Jack be nimble,
And Jack be quick;
And Jack jump over
The candlestick.

Ask your Grocer for STAR SOAP.

6

Goosey, goosey,
gander,
Where shall I wan-
der?
Up stairs, down stairs,
And in my lady's
chamber:
There I met an old
man,
Who would not say
his prayers,
Took him by the left
leg,
And threw him
down stairs.

STAR ★ SOAP

BEST FOR FAMILY USE.

STAR SOAP—The Perfection of Family Soaps.

7

There was an old woman
Lived under the hill,
And if she's not gone
She lives there still.

If you want white clothes use STAR SOAP.

10

There was an
old woman
who lived in
a shoe,
She had so
many child-
ren she didn't
know what to
do.

She gave them some broth,
without any bread;
She whipped them all soundly,
and put them to bed.

Live Grocers sell STAR SOAP.

Another form of advertising for companies was the little booklet. This spread features examples of a nursery-rhyme booklet distributed by the Star Soap Company.

Still another form, which is not shown on these pages, is the children's play set. This included a few pieces, similar to paper dolls, depicting a particular nursery rhyme.

Victorian Trade Card Booklet

Star Soap Co.
ca. 1890
Artist: unknown

My mother always uses STAR SOAP at home.

STAR SOAP has come to stay.

Try STAR SOAP and you will use no other.

STAR SOAP has no Superior.

For instance, one might portray Old King Cole as the main figure, one separate piece might be his throne, and another piece might depict his fiddler's three. These are hard to find with all the pieces intact.

Sing a song of sixpence, a pocket full of rye;
Four and twenty Blackbirds baked in a pie.
When the pie was opened, the birds began to sing,
Was not that a dainty dish to set before the King?

Vintage postcard
Trademark of an eagle
ca. 1910
Artist: unknown

Jack and Jill went up the hill
To fetch a pail of water.
Jack fell down and broke his crown
And Jill came tumbling after!

Vintage postcard
C. W. Faulkner & Co. Ltd., London E.C.
Series 1234
ca. 1910-1915
Artist: H.G.C. Marsh

BAA, BAA, BLACK SHEEP
HAVE YOU ANY WOOL?
YES SIR, YES SIR, THREE BAGS FULL.
ONE FOR MY MASTER, ONE FOR MY DAME,
BUT NONE FOR THE LITTLE GIRL
WHO CRIES IN THE LANE.

402

COPYRIGHTED 1907 BY JULIUS BIEN & CO. N.Y.

"BAA, BAA, BLACK SHEEP"

Vintage postcard
Julius Bien & Co., NY, 1907
Nursery Rhyme Series, Number 40
Artist: unknown

EARLY POSTCARDS

Picture postcards have been collectibles since the early 1900s. The name for this hobby is deltiology, and postcards are considered one of the three largest collectible items in the world, coin and stamp collectibles are the other two. The Golden Age of postcards was from 1898 to 1918.

The earliest postcards, as far as fairy tales and nursery rhymes were concerned, came out in Europe between 1895 and 1900. They were of fairy tales. The nursery-rhyme postcards started to appear in England and the United States in the early 1900s. Early twentieth-century nursery-rhyme postcards are represented in this section.

There were many series of nursery-rhyme cards issued by several postcard companies. As in the early Mother Goose books in the late nineteenth and early twentieth centuries, the artists were not always recognized on the postcards. The postcards with the gold fancy borders on these pages are a series that can be found fairly easy on Internet auction sites. "Baa, Baa, Black Sheep" is the oldest one in my collection.

Between 1901 and 1907, the backs of postcards were required to have only the address, no messages. They were undivided opposed to picture postcards of today which are divided. Therefore, the only place people could write a message was on the front where the picture was. This, of course, took away from the beautiful images. In 1907, the government allowed postcard companies to go to a divided back, half for a message and half for the address. This way the picture was not damaged by the written messages. All the nursery-rhyme postcards in this section have divided backs.

Vintage postcard
Trademark of an eagle
ca. 1910
Artist: unknown

Vintage postcard
Trademark of an eagle
ca. 1910
Artist: unknown

Vintage postcard
National Art Company
copyrighted 1906
Artist: unknown

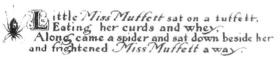

ittle *Miss Muffett* sat on a tuffett.
Eating her curds and whey,
Along came a spider and sat down beside her
and frightened *Miss Muffett* away.

311

Vintage postcard
National Art Company
ca. 1910
Artist: unknown

ittle *Jack Horner* sat in a corner.
Eating a Christmas pie;
He put in his thumb and pulled out a plum,
And said what a *Good Boy* am I!

310

Book cover
Gems from Mother Goose
Polly Put the Kettle On
McLoughlin Bros., NY, 1899
Artist: unknown

RHYME TIME

Mother Goose's Nursery Rhymes
Ernest Nister, London
E.P. Dutton & Co., NY, n.d.
Artist: unknown

Mother Goose's Nursery Rhymes
Graham & Matlack, NY, ca. 1915
Artist: unknown

The Complete Mother Goose
Frederick A. Stokes Co., 1909
Artist: Ethel Franklin Betts

OLD MOTHER GOOSE

Old Mother Goose
When she wanted to wander,
Would ride through the air
On a very fine gander.

Little Miss Muffet and Other Stories
McLoughlin Bros., NY, 1902
Artist: unknown

Mother Goose in Song and Rhyme
Charles E. Graham & Co., 1930
Artist: Clara Miller Burd

Mother Goose had a house,
'Twas built in a wood,
Where an owl at the door
For sentinel stood.

She had a son Jack,
A plain-looking lad,
He was not very good,
Nor yet very bad.

She sent him to market—
A live goose he bought:
"Here, mother," says he,
"It will not go for naught."

"Mother Goose and son Jack"

Mother Goose's Nursery Rhymes
McLoughlin Bros., NY, n.d.
Artist: unknown

Jack's goose and her gander
Grew very fond,
They'd both eat together,
Or swim in one pond.

Jack found one fine morning,
As I have been told,
His goose had laid him
An egg of pure gold.

Jack rode to his mother,
The news for to tell;
She called him a good boy
And said it was well.

Jack sold his gold egg
To a rascally knave,
Not half of its value
To poor Jack he gave.

Then Jack went a-courting
A lady so gay,
As fair as the lily,
And sweet as the May.

The knave and the Squire
Came up at his back,
And began to belabor
The sides of poor Jack.

And then the gold egg
Was thrown into the sea,
When Jack he jumped in,
And got it back presently.

The knave got the goose,
Which he vowed he would kill,
Resolving at once
His pockets to fill.

Jack's mother came in
And caught the goose soon,
And mounting its back,
Flew up to the moon.

Mother Goose's Nursery Rhymes
McLoughlin Bros., NY, n.d.
Artist: unknown

Mother Goose Her Own Book
The Reilly & Lee Co.
E. M. Kovar, 1932
Artist: Mary Royt

OLD
KING
COLE

Mother Goose's Rhymes
Frederick Warne & Co., n.d.
Artist: unknown

The Baby's Opera
McLoughlin Bros., NY, n.d.
Artist: Walter Crane

Mother Goose Chimes
McLoughlin Bros., NY, ca. 1880
Artist: unknown

Old King Cole was a merry old soul,
And a merry old soul was he;
He called for his pipe,
And he called for his bowl,
And he called for his fiddlers three.

"Old King Cole"
Mother Goose Rhymes
The Platt & Munk Co., Inc., 1927
Artist: Clara Miller Burd

POLLY PUT THE KETTLE ON

Polly, put the kettle on,   Sukey, take it off again,
Polly, put the kettle on,   Sukey, take it off again,
Polly, put the kettle on,   Sukey, take it off again,
And let's drink tea.   They're all gone away.

NEEDLES AND PINS

Needles and Pins,
Needles and Pins,
When a man marries,
His trouble begins.

Mother Goose's Nursery Rhymes
McLoughlin Bros., NY, n.d.
Artist: unknown

BYE, BABY BUNTING

Bye, baby bunting,
Daddy's gone a hunting,
To get a little rabbit skin
To wrap baby bunting in.

A SUNSHINY SHOWER

A sunshiny shower
Won't last half an hour.

THIS IS THE WAY WE MAKE THE HAY

Mother Goose's Nursery Rhymes
Ernest Nister, E. P. Dutton & Co., n.d.
Artist: unknown

This is the way we make the hay,
Make the hay, make the hay,
This is the way we make the hay,
All on a summer's morning.

OLD MOTHER HUBBARD

Old Mother Hubbard
Went to the cupboard,
To fetch her poor dog a bone;
But when she got there
The cupboard was bare
And so the poor dog had none.

Mother Goose Melodies
DeWolfe, Fiske & Co., n.d.
Artist: unknown

Mother Goose
McLoughlin Bros., NY, 1907
Artist: unknown

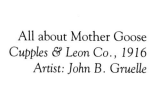

All about Mother Goose
Cupples & Leon Co., 1916
Artist: John B. Gruelle

SEE SAW, MARGERY DAW

The Complete Mother Goose
Frederick A. Stokes Co., 1909
Artist: Ethel Franklin Betts

See saw, Margery Daw,
Johnny shall have a new master;
He shall have but a penny a day,
Because he can't work any faster.

Old Fashioned Mother Goose Rhymes & Tales
Albert Whitman & Co., n.d.
Artist: unknown

SIMPLE SIMON

Simple Simon met a pieman,
Going to the fair;
Says Simple Simon to the pieman,
"Let me taste your ware."

Says the pieman to Simple Simon
"Show me first your penny,"
Says Simple Simon to the pieman,
"Indeed I have not any."

A Tiny Book of Nursery Rhyme
from Mother Goose
The Harter Publishing Co., 1934
Artist: Chester Van Nortwick

The Old Mother Goose Nursery Rhyme Book
Thomas Nelson & Sons, 1926
Artist: Anne Anderson

Mother Goose Melodies
DeWolfe, Fiske & Co., n.d.
Artist: undecernable

Simple Simon went a-hunting,
For to catch a hare,
He rode an ass about the streets
But couldn't find one there.

He went to shoot a wild duck,
But wild duck flew away;
Says Simon, I can't hit him,
Because he will not stay.

He went to ride a spotted cow
That had a little calf,
She threw him down upon the
    ground,
Which made the people laugh.

Once Simon made a great
    snow-ball
And brought it in to roast;
He laid it down before the fire,
And soon the ball was lost.

Simon he to market went,
To buy a joint of meat;
He tied it to his horse's tail
To keep it clean and sweet.

He went for to eat honey
Out of the mustard-pot,
He bit his tongue until he
    cried—
That was all the good he got.

Simple Simon went a-fishing
For to catch a whale;
All the water he had got
Was in his mother's pail.

He went for water in a sieve,
But soon it all run through,
And now poor Simple Simon
Bids you all Adieu.

THREE WISE MEN OF GOTHAM

Three wise men of Gotham
Went to sea in a bowl.
If the bowl had been stronger,
My song would be longer.

WE ARE ALL IN THE DUMPS

We are all in the dumps,
For diamonds are trumps;
The kittens have gone to St. Pauls;
The babies are bit,
The moon's in a fit,
And the houses are built without walls.

HIGH DIDDLE DOUBT

High diddle doubt,
My candle's out,
My little maid's not at home;
Saddle my hog,
And bridle my dog,
And fetch my little maid home.

"Three Wise Men of Gotham"

Mother Goose
McLoughlin Bros., NY, 1907
Artist: unknown

DANCE, LITTLE BABY, DANCE UP HIGH

Dance, little baby, dance up high,
Never mind, baby, mother is by;
Crow and caper, caper and crow,
There, little baby, there you go;

Up to the ceiling, down to the ground,
Backwards and forwards, round and round
Dance, little baby, and mother will sing
With the merry carol, ding, ding, ding!

JACK BE NIMBLE

Jack be nimble,
Jack be quick,
Jack jump over
the candlestick.

Gems from Mother Goose
Rhymes, Chimes and Jingles
McLoughlin Bros., 1898
Artist: unknown

THREE STRAWS ON A STAFF

Three straws on a staff,
Would make a baby
Cry and laugh.

"Dance, Little Baby, Dance Up High"

Gems from Mother Goose
Rhymes, Chimes and Jingles
McLoughlin Bros., 1898
Artist: unknown

THERE WAS AN OLD WOMAN
WHO LIVED IN A SHOE

Mother Goose Melodies
DeWolfe, Fiske & Co., n.d.
Artist: unknown

Tommy Tucker's Mother Goose Melodies
McLoughlin Bros., NY, 1887
Artist: unknown

There was an old woman who
  lived in a shoe.
She had so many children she
  didn't know what to do;
She gave them some broth
  without any bread;
She whipped them all soundly
  and put them to bed.

Little Miss Muffet and Other Stories
McLoughlin Bros., NY, 1902
Artist: unknown

"Old Woman Who Lived in a Shoe"

The Ella Dolbear Lee Mother Goose
M. A. Donohue & Co., 1918
Artist: Ella Dolbear Lee

ELIZABETH, ELIZA, BETSY, AND BESS

Elizabeth, Eliza, Betsy, and Bess,
All went together to seek a bird's nest.
They found a bird's nest with five eggs in it,
They all took one and left four in it.

TWEEDLE-DUM AND TWEEDLE-DEE

Gems from Mother Goose
Rhymes, Chimes and Jingles
McLoughlin Bros., 1898
Artist: unknown

Tweedle-Dum and
  Tweedle-Dee
Resolved to have a
  battle.
For Tweedle-Dum said
  Tweedle-Dee
Had spoiled his nice
  new rattle.
Just then flew by a
  monstrous crow,
As big as a tar barrel,
Which frightened both
  the heroes so,
They quite forgot their
  quarrel.

"Elizabeth, Eliza, Betsy, and Bess"

Gems from Mother Goose
Rhymes, Chimes and Jingles
McLoughlin Bros., 1898
Artist: unknown

LITTLE BOY BLUE

Mother Goose's Nursery Rhymes
Ernest Nister, E.P. Dutton & Co., n.d.
Artist: unknown

Little Boy Blue
Come blow your horn,
The sheep's in the meadow,
The cow's in the corn.

Where is the boy
Who looks after the sheep?
He's under a haystack
Fast asleep.

Will you wake him?
No, not I,
For if I do,
He's sure to cry.

Mother Goose Melodies
DeWolfe, Fiske & Co., n.d.
Artist: unknown

"Little Boy Blue"

Mother Goose's Rhymes
Frederick Warne & Co., n.d.
Artist: unknown

DING, DONG BELL

Ding, dong bell,
Pussy's in the well.
Who put her in?

Little Tommy Green,
Who pulled her out?
Little Tommy Stout.

HUSHY, BABY, MY DOLL

Hushy, baby, my doll,
I pray you don't cry,
And I'll give you some bread
And some milk by and by;
Or perhaps you like custard,
Or maybe a tart—
Then to either you're welcome,
With all my whole heart.

Mother Goose's Nursery Rhymes
Ernest Nister, E.P. Dutton & Co., n.d.
Artist: unknown

"Ding, Dong Bell"

Mother Goose's Rhymes
Frederick Warne & Co., n.d.
Artist: unknown

"As I Was Going Up Pippin Hill"

Gems from Mother Goose
Rhymes, Chimes and Jingles
McLoughlin Bros., NY, 1898
Artist: unknown

AS I WAS GOING UP PIPPIN HILL

As I was going up Pippin Hill,
Pippin Hill was dirty;
There I met a pretty Miss,
And she dropped me a curtsy.

Little Miss, pretty Miss,
Blessings light upon you;
If I had half a crown a day,
I'd spend it all upon you.

THERE WAS AN OLD WOMAN

There was an old woman who
  rode on a broom,
With a heigh, gee-ho, gee-humble.
And she took her old cat behind
  for a groom,
With a bumble, bumble, bumble.

Gems from Mother Goose
Rhymes, Chimes and Jingles
McLoughlin Bros., NY, 1898
Artist: unknown

LITTLE TOMMY TUCKER

Little Tommy Tucker
Sings for his supper;
What shall we give him?
White bread and butter.
How shall he cut it
Without e'er a knife?
How will he be married
Without e'er a wife?

Mother Goose's Rhymes
Frederick Warne & Co., n.d.
Artist: unknown

MARY HAD A LITTLE LAMB

Mary had a little lamb,
Its fleece was white as snow;
And everywhere that Mary went
The lamb was sure to go.

Mother Goose Nursery Rhymes
Sam'l Gabriel Sons & Co., 1915
Artist: A. M. Turner

Mother Goose Melodies
DeWolfe, Fiske & Co., n.d.
Artist: unknown

It followed her to school one day,
That was against the rule;
It made the children laugh and play
To see a lamb at school.

Mother Goose's Nursery Rhymes
Ernest Nister, E.P. Dutton & Co., n.d.
Artist: unknown

"The Old Woman Who Lived on Victuals and Drink"

Mother Goose
McLoughlin Bros., NY, 1907
Artist: unknown

THERE WAS AN OLD WOMAN

There was an old woman, and what do you think?
She lived upon nothing but victuals and drink;
Victuals and drink were the chief of her diet,
Yes, this tiresome woman could never be quiet.

PEASE PORRIDGE HOT

Gems from Mother Goose
Rhymes, Chimes and Jingles
McLoughlin Bros., NY, 1898
Artist: unknown

Pease porridge hot,
Pease porridge cold,
Pease porridge in the pot,
Nine days old.

Some like it hot,
Some like it cold,
Some like it in the pot,
Nine days old.

THE MAN IN THE MOON

The man in the moon
Came tumbling down,
And asked his way to Norwich;
He went by the south,
And burnt his mouth,
With supping cold pease-porridge.

BIRDS OF A FEATHER FLOCK TOGETHER

Birds of a feather flock together,
And so will pigs and swine,
Rats and mice will have their choice,
And so will I have mine.

SNEEZE ON MONDAY

Sneeze on Monday, sneeze for danger;
Sneeze on Tuesday, kiss a stranger;
Sneeze on Wednesday, receive a letter;
Sneeze on Thursday, something better;
Sneeze on Friday, expect sorrow;
Sneeze on Saturday, joy to-morrow.

"The Man in the Moon"

Mother Goose
McLoughlin Bros., NY, 1907
Artist: unknown

SING A SONG OF SIXPENCE

Sing a song of sixpence
A pocket full of rye;
Four and twenty blackbirds
Baked in a pie.

When the pie was opened
The birds began to sing;
Was not that a dainty dish,
To set before the King?

Mother Goose Chimes
McLoughlin Bros., NY, ca. 1880s
Artist: unknown

Mother Goose in Song and Rhyme
Charles E. Graham & Co., 1930
Artist: Clara Miller Burd

Riddles

AS I WAS GOING TO ST. IVES

As I was going to St. Ives,
I met a man with seven wives,
Every wife had seven sacks,
Every sack had seven cats,
Every cat had seven kits,—
Kits, cats, sacks, and wives,
How many were there going to St. Ives?
(one)

FORMED LONG AGO, YET MADE TODAY

Formed long ago, yet made today;
Employed while others sleep;
What few would like to give away,
Nor any wish to keep.
(a bed)

I WENT TO THE WOOD AND GOT IT

I went to the wood and got it;
I sat me down and looked at it;
The more I looked at it the less I liked it,
And I brought it home because I couldn't help it.
(a thorn)

THERE WAS AN OLD WOMAN

There was an old woman lived under the hill,
And if she's not gone, she lives there still.
Baked apples she sold, and cranberry pies,
And she's the old woman that never told lies.

ONCE I SAW A LITTLE BIRD

Once I saw a little bird
Come hop, hop, hop;
So I cried, "Little bird,
Will you stop, stop, stop?"
And I was going to the window
To say, "How do you do?"
But he shook his little tail,
And far away he flew.

GO TO BED FIRST

Go to bed first, a golden purse;
Go to bed second, a golden
  pheasant;
Go to bed third, a golden bird.

GREAT A, LITTLE a

Great A, little a, bouncing B,
The cat's in the cupboard,
And she can't see.

PAT-A-CAKE, PAT-A-CAKE

Mother Goose Rhymes
The Platt & Munk Co., Inc., 1927
Artist: Clara Miller Burd

Pat-a-cake, pat-a-cake, baker's man.
Bake me a cake as fast as you can.
Pat it and roll it and mark it with a B.
And put it in the oven for baby and me.

LITTLE MISS MUFFET

Little Miss Muffet
Sat on a tuffet,
Eating her curds
And whey;
There came a
Big spider,
Who sat down
Beside her
And frightened
Miss Muffet away.

Mother Goose's Rhymes
Frederick Warne & Co., n.d.
Artist: unknown

The Complete Mother Goose
Frederick A. Stokes Co., 1909
Artist: Ethel Franklin Betts

Mother Goose's Nursery Rhymes
Ernest Nister, E.P. Dutton & Co., n.d.
Artist: unknown

HICKETY, PICKETY, MY BLACK HEN

Mother Goose Rhymes
Frederick Warne & Co., n.d.
Artist: unknown

Old Fashioned Mother Goose Rhymes and Tales
Albert Whitman & Co., Chicago, n.d.
Artist: Henley

Mother Goose Nursery Rhymes
Ernest Nister, E.P. Dutton & Co., n.d.
Artist: unknown

Hickety, pickety,
My black hen,
She lays eggs
For gentlemen;
Gentlemen come
Every day
To see what my
Black hen doth lay.

JACK SPRAT

Jack Sprat could eat no fat,
His wife could eat no lean.
And so betwixt them both, you see,
They licked the platter clean.

Mother Goose Her Own Book
The Reilly & Lee Co.
E. M. Kovar, 1932
Artist: Mary Royt

LITTLE JACK HORNER

Little Jack Horner
Sat in the corner,
Eating a Christmas pie;
He put in his thumb,
And pulled out a plum,
And said,
What a good boy am I!

The Complete Mother Goose
Frederick A. Stokes Co., 1909
Artist: Ethel Franklin Betts

Mother Goose's Nursery Rhymes
Graham & Matlack, n.d.
Artist: unknown

Mother Goose's Christmas Tour
McLoughlin Bros., NY, 1906
Artist: unknown

ONE, TWO, BUCKLE MY SHOE

Old Mother Goose's Rhymes & Tales
Frederick Warne & Co., 1889
Artist: Constance Haslewood

One, two, buckle my shoe,
Three, four, knock at the door,
Five, six, pick up sticks,
Seven, eight, lay them straight,
Nine, ten, a good fat hen,
Eleven, twelve, who will delve,
Thirteen, fourteen, maids a-courting,
Fifteen, sixteen, maids a-kissing,
Seventeen, eighteen, maids a-waiting,
Nineteen, twenty, give me plenty.

ONE, TWO, THREE, FOUR, FIVE

One, two, three, four, five,
I caught a fish alive;
Six, seven, eight, nine, ten,
I let it go again.

*Gems from Mother Goose
Rhymes, Chimes and Jingles
McLoughlin Bros., NY, 1898
Artist: unknown*

RIDE A COCK-HORSE
TO SHREWSBURY CROSS

Little Miss Muffet and Other Stories
McLoughlin Bros., NY, 1902
Artist: unknown

Ride a cock-horse to Shrewsbury cross,
To buy little Johnny a galloping horse:
It trots behind, and it ambles before,
And Johnny shall ride—till he can ride no more.

RUB-A-DUB-DUB

Little Miss Muffet and Other Stories
McLoughlin Bros., NY, 1902
Artist: unknown

Rub-a-dub-dub, three men in a tub,
The butcher, the baker, the candlestick-maker,
All jumped out of a rotten potato.

HEY DIDDLE, DIDDLE

Hey diddle, diddle,
  the cat and the fiddle,
The cow jumped
  over the moon;
The little dog laughed
  to see such sport,
And the dish ran away
  with the spoon.

Mother Goose in Song and Rhyme
Charles E. Graham & Co., 1930
Artist: Clara Miller Burd

Mother Goose's Nursery Rhymes
Ernest Nister, E.P. Dutton & Co., n.d.
Artist: unknown

Riddles

IN MARBLE WALLS AS WHITE AS MILK

In marble walls as white as milk,
Lined with a skin as soft as silk;
Within a fountain crystal clear,
A golden apple doth appear.
No doors there are to this stronghold—
Yet thieves break in and steal the gold.
(an egg)

LITTLE NANCY ETTICOTE

Little Nancy Etticote
In a white petticoat,
With a red nose:
The longer she stands,
The shorter she grows.
(a candle)

A RIDDLE, A RIDDLE, AS I SUPPOSE

A riddle, a riddle, as I suppose,
A hundred eyes, and never a nose.
(a cinder-sifter)

YOUNG LAMBS TO SELL!

Mother Goose Rhymes
Frederick Warne & Co., n.d.
Artist: unknown

Young lambs to sell!
Young lambs to sell!
If I'd as much money as I can tell,
I never would cry young lambs to sell!

THE COCK'S ON THE HOUSETOP

The cock's on the housetop blowing his horn;
The bull's in the barn a-threshing of corn;
The maids in the meadows are making of hay;
The ducks in the river are swimming away.

THE QUEEN OF HEARTS

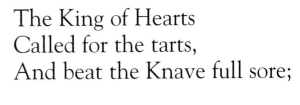

The Queen of Hearts,
She made some tarts,
All on a summer's day;

The Knave of Hearts,
He stole those tarts,
And took them clean away.

The King of Hearts
Called for the tarts,
And beat the Knave full sore;

The Knave of Hearts
Brought back the tarts,
And vowed he'd steal no more.

Mother Goose Melodies
DeWolfe, Fiske & Co., n.d.
Artist: unknown

MULTIPLICATION IS VEXATION

Mother Goose's Nursery Rhymes
Ernest Nister, E.P. Dutton & Co., n.d.
Artist: unknown

Multiplication is vexation,
Division is just as bad;
The Rule of Three perplexes me,
And practice drives me mad.

JACKY

"Jacky, come give me your fiddle,
If ever you mean to thrive."
"Nay, I'll not give my fiddle
To any man alive."

"If I should give my fiddle,
They'll think that I've gone mad;
For many a joyful day
My fiddle and I have had."

Gems from Mother Goose
Rhymes, Chimes and Jingles
McLoughlin Bros., NY, 1898
Artist: unknown

LITTLE BOYS

Whenever the moon begins to peep,
Little boys should be asleep;
The great big sun shines all the day,
That little boys can see to play.

THE FIVE LITTLE PIGGIES

This little pig went to market,
This little pig stayed at home,
This little pig had roast beef,
This little pig had none,
This little pig cried wee, wee,
  wee, all the way home.

Mother Goose's Rhymes
Frederick Warne & Co., n.d.
Artist: unknown

GIRLS AND BOYS, COME OUT TO PLAY

Girls and boys, come out to play,
The moon doth shine as bright as day;
Leave your supper, and leave your sleep,
And come with your playfellows into the street.
Come and a whoop, come with a call,
Come with a good will or not at all.
Up the ladder and down the wall,
A half-penny roll will serve us all.
You find milk, and I'll find flour,
And we'll have a pudding in half an hour.

ROBERT BARNES

"Robert Barnes, fellow fine,
Can you shoe this horse of mine?"
"Yes, good sir, that I can,
As well as any other man:
Here a nail, and there a prod,
And now, good sir,
Your horse is shod."

Gems from Mother Goose
Rhymes, Chimes and Jingles
McLoughlin Bros., NY, 1898
Artist: unknown

"There Was a Man in Our Town"

Mother Goose
McLoughlin Bros., NY, 1907
Artist: unknown

THERE WAS A MAN IN OUR TOWN

There was a man in our town,
And he was wondrous wise;
He jumped into a bramble bush
And scratched out both his eyes.

And when he saw his eyes were out,
With all his might and main,
He jumped into another bush
And scratched them in again.

INTERY, MINTERY, CUTERY CORN

Intery, mintery, cutery corn,
Apple seed, and apple thorn;
Wine, brier, limber lock,
Three geese in a flock,
One flew east, and one flew west,
And one flew over the goose's nest.

Gems from Mother Goose
Rhymes, Chimes and Jingles
McLoughlin Bros., NY, 1898
Artist: unknown

HERE AM I

Here am I, little jumping Joan
When nobody's with me,
I am always alone.

JANUARY BRINGS THE SNOW

January brings the snow,
Makes our feet and fingers glow.

February brings the rain,
Thaws the frozen lake again.

March brings breezes loud and shrill,
Stirs the dancing daffodil.

April brings the primrose sweet,
Scatters daisies at our feet.

May brings flocks of pretty lambs,
Skipping by their fleecy dams.

June brings tulips, lilies, roses,
Fills the children's hands with posies.

Hot July brings cooling showers
Apricots and gillyflowers.

August brings the sheaves of corn,
Then the harvest home is borne.

Warm September brings the fruit,
Sportsmen then begin to shoot.

Fresh October brings the pheasant,
Then to gather nuts is pleasant.

Dull November brings the blast,
Then the leaves are whirling fast.

Chill December brings the sleet,
Blazing fire and Christmas treat.

THE NORTH WIND DOTH BLOW

The north wind doth blow,
And we shall have snow,
And what will the children do then,
Poor things?

When lessons are done,
They'll jump, skip, and run,
And that's how they'll keep themselves warm,
Poor things.

Mother Goose's Nursery Rhymes
Ernest Nister, E.P. Dutton & Co., n.d.
Artist: unknown

HOT CROSS BUNS

Hot cross buns,
Hot cross buns,
One a penny, two a penny,
Hot cross buns.
If your daughters
Don't like them,
Give them to your sons.
One a penny, two a penny,
Hot cross buns.

Gems from Mother Goose
Rhymes, Chimes and Jingles
McLoughlin Bros., NY, 1898
Artist: unknown

THIRTY DAYS HATH SEPTEMBER

Thirty days hath September,
April, June and November;
All the rest have thirty-one—
Except February, alone,
Which has four and twenty-four,
And every fourth year, one day more.

TOMMY SNOOKS AND BESSY BROOKS

As Tommy Snooks and Bessy Brooks
Were walking out one Sunday,
Says Tommy Snooks to Bessy Brooks
"Tomorrow will be Monday."

Gems from Mother Goose
Rhymes, Chimes and Jingles
McLoughlin Bros., NY, 1898
Artist: unknown

I HAD A LITTLE NUT TREE

Gems from Mother Goose
Rhymes, Chimes and Jingles
McLoughlin Bros., NY, 1898
Artist: unknown

I had a little nut tree, nothing would it bear
But a silver apple and a golden pear.
The King of Spain's daughter came to visit me,
And all for the sake of my little nut tree.
I skipped over water, I danced over sea,
And all the birds in the air couldn't catch me.

HUMPTY DUMPTY

Old Fashioned Mother Goose
Rhymes and Tales
Albert Whitman & Co., n.d.
Artist: unknown

Gems from Mother Goose
Rhymes, Chimes and Jingles
McLoughlin Bros., NY, 1898
Artist: unknown

Humpty Dumpty sat on a wall,
Humpty Dumpty had a great fall;
All the King's horses and
   all the King's men
Couldn't put Humpty
   together again.

The Ella Dolbear Lee Mother Goose
M. A. Donohue & Co., 1918
Artist: Ella Dolbear Lee

RING-A-RING-A-ROSES

Ring-a-ring-a-roses,
A pocketful of posies;
Hush-hush-hush-hush
We'll all tumble down.

Mother Goose's Nursery Rhymes
Ernest Nister, E.P. Dutton & Co., n.d.
Artist: unknown

HERE WE GO ROUND THE MULBERRY BUSH

Here we go round the mulberry bush,
The mulberry bush, the mulberry bush,
Here we go round the mulberry bush,
On a cold and frosty morning.

This is the way we wash our hands,
Wash our hands, wash our hands,
This is the way we wash our hands,
On a cold and frosty morning.

This is the way we wash our clothes,
Wash our clothes, wash our clothes,
This is the way we wash our clothes,
On a cold and frosty morning.

This is the way we go to school,
Go to school, go to school,
This is the way we go to school,
On a cold and frosty morning.

Gems from Mother Goose
Rhymes, Chimes and Jingles
McLoughlin Bros., NY, 1898
Artist: unknown

LITTLE BETTY BLUE

Little Betty Blue
Lost her holiday shoe;
What can little Betty do?

Give her another
To match the other,
And then she may walk in two.

BARBER, BARBER, SHAVE A PIG

Barber, barber, shave a pig,
How many hairs will make a wig?
"Four and twenty, that's enough,"
Give the poor barber a pinch of snuff.

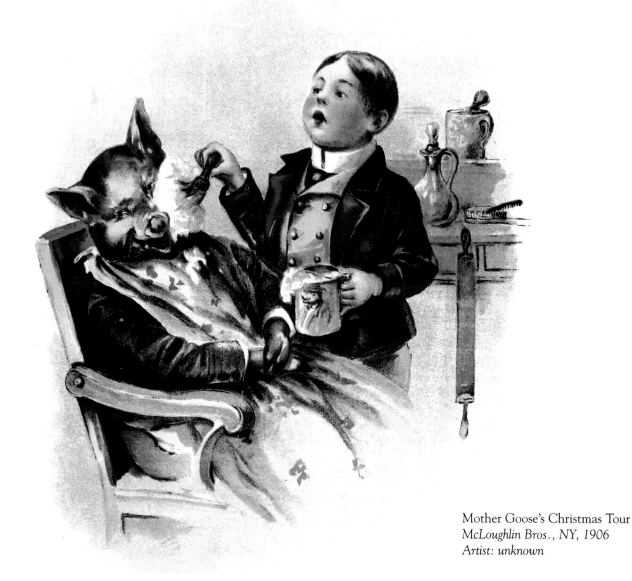

Mother Goose's Christmas Tour
McLoughlin Bros., NY, 1906
Artist: unknown

TO MARKET, TO MARKET

Mother Goose's Rhymes
Frederick Warne & Co., n.d.
Artist: unknown

To market, to market,
To buy a fat pig,
Home again, home again,
Jiggety-jig.

To market, to market,
To buy a fat hog,
Home again, home again,
Jiggety-jog.

GATHERING NUTS AND MAY

Here we come gathering nuts
    and may,
Nuts and may,
Nuts and may;
Here we come gathering nuts
    and may.
On a cold and frosty morning.

> May is the name of the
> blossom of the Hawthorn.

Little Miss Muffet and Other Stories
McLoughlin Bros., NY, 1902
Artist: unknown

Mother Goose's Nursery Rhymes
Ernest Nister, E.P. Dutton & Co., n.d.
Artist: unknown

CROSS PATCH

Gems from Mother Goose
Rhymes, Chimes and Jingles
McLoughlin Bros., NY, 1898
Artist: unknown

Cross patch,
Draw the latch,
Sit by the fire and spin;

Take a cup
And drink it up,
Then call your neighbors in.

JACK AND JILL

Mother Goose's Rhymes
Frederick Warne & Co., n.d.
Artist: unknown

The Complete Mother Goose
Frederick A. Stokes Co., 1909
Artist: Ethel Franklin Betts

Jack and Jill went up the hill
To fetch a pail of water;
Jack fell down and broke his crown
And Jill came tumbling after.

Up Jack got and home did trot
As fast as he could caper;
To old Dame Dob,
Who patched his nob
With vinegar and brown paper.

Mother Goose Melodies
DeWolfe, Fiske & Co., n.d.
Artist: unknown

HANDY SPANDY

Handy spandy, Jack-a-dandy
Loves plum-cake and sugar candy;
He bought some at a grocer's shop
And out he came, hop-hop-hop.

Gems from Mother Goose
Rhymes, Chimes and Jingles
McLoughlin Bros., NY, 1898
Artist: unknown

MILKMAN, MILKMAN

"Milkman, milkman, where have you been?"
"In Buttermilk Channel, up to my chin:
I spilt my milk, and spoiled my clothes,
And got a long icicle hung to my nose!"

DOCTOR FOSTER

Doctor Foster went to Gloster,
In a shower of rain;
He stepped in a puddle
Up to the middle,
And never went there again.

Gems from Mother Goose
Rhymes, Chimes and Jingles
McLoughlin Bros., NY, 1898
Artist: unknown

LITTLE JACK DANDY-PRAT

Little Jack Dandy-prat was my first suitor;
He'd a dish and a spoon and he'd some pewter;
He'd linen and woolen, and woolen and linen;
A little pig in a string cost him five shilling.

PUSSYCAT, PUSSYCAT

Mother Goose Rhymes
Frederick Warne & Co., n.d.
Artist: unknown

Pussycat, pussycat, where have you been?
I've been up to London to look at the Queen.
Pussycat, pussycat, what did you there?
I frightened a little mouse under her chair.

RIDE A COCK-HORSE TO BANBURY CROSS

Mother Goose's Nursery Rhymes
Ernest Nister, E.P. Dutton & Co., n.d.
Artist: unknown

Ride a cock-horse
    to Banbury Cross
To see a fine Lady
    upon a white horse;
Rings on her fingers
    and bells on her toes,
And she shall have
    music wherever
    she goes.

Mother Goose's Rhymes
Frederick Warne & Co., n.d.
Artist: unknown

ROCK-A-BYE BABY

Rock-a-bye baby,
On the tree top,
When the wind blows
The cradle will rock;
When the bough breaks
The cradle will fall,
Down will come baby,
Cradle, and all.

Mother Goose's Nursery Rhymes
Ernest Nister, E.P. Dutton & Co., n.d.
Artist: unknown

Gems from Mother Goose
Rhymes, Chimes and Jingles
McLoughlin Bros., NY, 1898
Artist: unknown

Mother Goose's Rhymes
Frederick Warne & Co., n.d.
Artist: unknown

PETER, PETER, PUMPKIN EATER

Peter, Peter, pumpkin eater,
Had a wife and couldn't keep her;
He put her in a pumpkin shell
And there he kept her very well.

A Tiny Book of Nursery Rhymes from Mother Goose
The Harter Publishing Company, 1934
Artist: Chester Van Nortwick

Jessie Willcox Smith Mother Goose
Good Housekeeping Magazine, *1914*
Artist: Jessie Willcox Smith

"Peter, Peter, Pumpkin Eater"

Mother Goose
McLoughlin Bros., NY, 1907
Artist: unknown

TOM HE WAS A PIPER'S SON

The Fanny Cory Mother Goose
The Bobbs-Merrill Co., 1913
Artist: Fanny Y. Cory

Tom he was a piper's son,
He learned to play
   when he was young.
But all the tunes that
   he could play,
Was "Over the hills and far away."

Now, Tom with his pipe made such a noise,
That he pleased both the girls and boys,
And they all stopped to hear him play,
Was "Over the hills and far away."

Tom with his pipe did play with such skill,
That those who heard him could never stand still;
Whenever they heard him they began to dance—
Even the pigs on their hind legs would after him prance.

He met Old Dame Trot with a basket of eggs,
He used his pipe and she used her legs;
She danced about till the eggs were all broke;
She began to fret, but he laughed at the joke.

He saw a cross fellow was beating an ass,
Heavy laden with pots, pans, dishes and glass;
He took out his pipe and played them a tune,
And the jackass's load was lightened full soon.

Mother Goose's Nursery Rhymes
Ernest Nister, E.P. Dutton & Co., n.d.
Artist: unknown

"There Was an Old Woman Tossed Up in a Basket"

Gems from Mother Goose
Rhymes, Chimes and Jingles
McLoughlin Bros., NY, 1898
Artist: unknown

THERE WAS AN OLD WOMAN

There was an old woman tossed up in a basket,
Nineteen times as high as the moon;
Where she was going I couldn't but ask it,
For in her hand she carried a broom.
Old woman, old woman, old woman, quoth I,
Where are you going to up so high?
To brush the cobwebs off the sky!
May I go with you? Aye, by-and-by.

IF ALL THE WORLD WAS APPLE-PIE

If all the world was apple-pie,
And all the sea was ink,
And all the trees were bread and cheese,
What should we have for drink?

DEEDLE, DEEDLE, DUMPLING

Deedle, deedle, dumpling, my son John,
He went to bed with his stockings on;
One shoe off, and one shoe on,
Deedle, deedle, dumpling, my son John.

THIS IS THE WAY THE LADIES RIDE

Mother Goose's Melodies
DeWolfe, Fiske & Co., n.d.
Artist: unknown

This is the way the ladies ride,
Tri, tre, tri, tree,
Tri, tre, tri, tree!
This is the way the ladies ride,
Tri, tre, tri, tree, tri, tre, tri, tree!

This is the way the gentlemen ride,
Gallop-a-trot,
Gallop-a-trot!
This is the way the gentlemen ride,
Gallop-a-trot-a-trot!

This is the way the farmers ride,
Hobbledy-hoy,
Hobbledy-hoy!
This is the way the farmers ride,
Hobbledy-hobbledy-hoy!

THERE WAS A LITTLE GIRL

There was a little girl,
And she had a little curl;
Right in the middle of
  her forehead;

When she was good
She was very, very good,
But when she was bad
  she was horrid.

CURLY LOCKS! CURLY LOCKS!

Curly locks! Curly locks!
Wilt thou be mine?
Thou shalt not wash dishes,
Nor yet feed the swine;
But sit on a cushion and
Sew a fine seam,
And feed upon strawberries,
Sugar and cream!

Mother Goose's Rhymes
Frederick Warne & Co., n.d.
Artist: unknown

Jessie Willcox Smith Mother Goose
Good Housekeeping Magazine, *1914*
Artist: Jessie Willcox Smith

HICKORY, DICKORY, DOCK

A Tiny Book of Nursery Rhymes from Mother Goose
The Harter Publishing Company, 1934
Artist: Chester Van Nortwick

Mother Goose Melodies
DeWolfe, Fiske & Co., n.d.
Artist: unknown

Hickory, dickory, dock,
The mouse ran up the clock,
The clock struck one
The mouse ran down,
Hickory, dickory, dock.

Mother Goose Melodies
DeWolfe, Fiske & Co., n.d.
Artist: unknown

PETER PIPER

Peter Piper picked
    a peck of pickled peppers.
A peck of pickled peppers
    Peter Piper picked;
If Peter Piper picked
    a peck of pickled peppers,
Where's the peck of pickled peppers
    Peter Piper picked?

Old Mother Goose's Nursery Rhymes
Graham & Matlack, n.d.
Artist: unknown

ONE, TWO, THREE, I LOVE COFFEE

One, two, three,
I love coffee,
And Billy loves tea.
How good you be!

One, two, three,
I love coffee,
And Billy loves tea.

Old Mother Goose's Nursery Rhymes
Graham & Matlack, n.d.
Artist: unknown

MISTRESS MARY, QUITE CONTRARY

Mistress Mary, quite contrary,
How does your garden grow?
With silver bells and cockle shells,
And pretty maids all in a row.

Mother Goose's Nursery Rhymes
Ernest Nister, E.P. Dutton & Co., n.d.
Artist: unknown

The Complete Mother Goose
Frederick A. Stokes Co., 1909
Artist: Ethel Franklin Betts

Mother Goose's Nursery Rhymes
Graham & Matlack, n.d.
Artist: unknown

BROW BRINKY

Brow brinky   Nose noppy,
Eye winkey,   Cheek cherry,
Chin choppy   Mouth merry.

MOLLIE, MY SISTER, AND I FELL OUT!

Mollie, my sister, and I fell out!
And what do you think it was about?
She loved coffee, and I loved tea,
And that was the reason
We couldn't agree.

HINX, MINX!

Hinx, minx! The old witch winks,
The fat begins to fry,
There's nobody home
But jumping Joan,
Father, mother and I.

Gems from Mother Goose
Rhymes, Chimes and Jingles
McLoughlin Bros., 1898
Artist: unknown

BAA, BAA, BLACK SHEEP

Mother Goose's Chimes
McLoughlin Bros., NY, n.d.
Artist: unknown

Baa, baa, black sheep
Have you any wool?
Yes, sir, yes, sir,
Three bags full;
One for my master,
And one for the dame,
And one for the little boy
Who lives on our lane.

Mother Goose's Nursery Rhymes
Ernest Nister, E.P. Dutton & Co., n.d.
Artist: unknown

MONDAY'S CHILD IS FAIR OF FACE

Monday's child is fair of face,
Tuesday's child is full of grace,
Wednesday's child is full of woe,
Thursday's child has far to go,
Friday's child is loving and giving,
Saturday's child works hard for its living,
And a child that's born on the Sabbath day,
Is fair and wise and good and gay.

WHERE ARE YOU GOING, MY PRETTY MAID

"Where are you going, my pretty maid?"
"I'm going a-milking, sir," she said.
            "May I go with you, my pretty maid?"
            "You're kindly welcome, sir," she said.
"What is your father, my pretty maid?"
"My father's a farmer, sir," she said.
            "What is your fortune, my pretty maid?"
            "My face is my fortune, sir," she said.
"Then I can't marry you, my pretty maid!"
"Nobody asked you, sir," she said.

LITTLE BO-PEEP

Little Bo-Peep has lost her sheep,
And doesn't know where to find them;
Leave them alone, and they'll come home,
Bringing their tails behind them.

A Tiny Book Of Nursery Rhymes
from Mother Goose
The Harter Publishing Company, 1934
Artist: Chester Van Nortwick

Mother Goose in Song and Rhyme
Charles E. Graham & Co., 1930
Artist: Clara Miller Burd

Little Bo-Peep fell fast asleep,
And dreamt she heard them bleating;
But when she woke, she found it a joke,
For they were still a-fleeting.

Mother Goose's Nursery Rhymes
Ernest Nister, E.P. Dutton, n.d.
Artist: unknown

"Little Bo-Peep"

Mother Goose's Rhymes
Frederick Warne & Co., n.d.
Artist: unknown

WHAT ARE LITTLE BOY'S MADE OF?

What are little boy's made of, made of,
What are little boy's made of?
Snaps and nails, and puppy-dogs' tails;
And that's what little boy's are made of, made of.

WHAT ARE LITTLE GIRLS MADE OF?

What are little girls made of, made of,
What are little girls made of?
Sugar and spice, and all that's nice;
And that's what little girls are made of, made of.

A MAN OF WORDS, AND NOT OF DEEDS

A man of words, and not of deeds,
Is like a garden full of weeds;
For when the weeds begin to grow,
Then doth the garden overflow.

WEE WILLIE WINKIE

Mother Goose Her Own Book
The Reilly & Lee Co.
E. M. Kovar, 1932
Artist: Mary Royt

Wee Willie Winkie
Runs through the town;
Upstairs and downstairs
In his nightgown,
Rapping at the window,
Crying through the lock,
"Are the children in their beds,
For its now eight o'clock?"

Mother Goose's Rhymes
Frederick Warne & Co., n.d.
Artist: unknown

RESOURCE GUIDE

Imagery of vintage postcards, trade cards, book, and newspaper illustrations are from the author's Mother Goose and nursery rhyme collection. All photography of imagery is by the author.

All illustrations are identified in this book as to their origin, the date if known, and who the artist is if known.

INDEX OF ARTISTS

Gems from Mother Goose
Rhymes, Chimes and Jingles
McLoughlin Bros., NY, 1898
Artist: unknown

INDEX OF NURSERY RHYMES BY FIRST LINES

Mother Goose's Rhymes
Frederick Warne & Co., n.d.
Artist: unknown